Matt Christopher

BASEBALL PALS

Little, Brown and Company
Boston   New York   London

ISBN 0-316-14005-8

Library of Congress Catalog Card No. 56-5920

20   19   18   17   16   15

COM

Printed in the United States of America

To my brothers

Fred
Mike
Tony
John
Rudy

and

Pop

BASEBALL PALS

1

Jimmie Todd brushed away a lock of brown hair from his forehead. He pounded his fist into his baseball glove and scowled at Johnny Lukon.

"Why can't I pitch?" he said. "I'm captain. We just voted on it, didn't we? And can't a captain play whatever position he wants to?"

"But you're no pitcher," said Johnny. He was a long-legged boy with brown eyes and fire-red hair. He was wearing a brand-new first-base mitt. "Why don't you let Paul pitch? He's a lefty, and lefties make good pitchers."

"Sure," said Alan Warzcak, sitting on one of the legs of the batting cage. He was small but could run faster and hit better than most boys his age. "You never pitched before. Let Paul pitch. He's taller than you and he has a good curve."

Jimmie clamped his teeth over his lower lip. His eyes darted fire. He thought of a lot of things he could call Johnny Lukon and Alan Warzcak. But he didn't. His younger brother, blue-eyed, sandy-haired Ervie, was standing beside him. He didn't want Ervie to go home and tell his mother he'd been quarreling with the boys on the ball diamond.

"I can pitch, too," Jimmie said stubbornly. "I've been practicing ever since the weather got warm."

Ervie's big blue eyes rolled around to him. Jimmie's ears reddened. Ervie was sort of chubby. He wore blue overalls that dragged at the heels of his shoes. He hardly ever said anything. His eyes always did the talking. Every time Jimmie told a fib, those eyes would look up at him, and Jimmie would feel guilty.

"Well, almost ever since then," Jimmie corrected himself.

The blue eyes rolled away. Ervie never even smiled.

"If we want a team in the Grasshoppers League, we'd better make up our minds now what positions we're going to play," said Jimmie. "I'll pitch. Johnny Lukon will play first base."

Then he turned to his best friend, Paul Karoski. Paul was the nicest kid he had ever known. He never said much. He never argued. He was the tallest one around, too. He was a good pitcher, although Jimmie thought that Paul would make a better first baseman. But now that Johnny Lukon had a first-base mitt, there was only the outfield for Paul to play.

"I know what you could play, Paul," Jimmie said, his eyes sparkling. "You can play the outfield, can't you?"

Paul shrugged. "Yes. I suppose so."

Jimmie's brows arched. "Will you?" he pleaded. "You can play center. That's where most of the flies are hit."

If he made Paul believe that playing center field was as important as pitching, maybe Paul wouldn't mind the change.

"If you say so," Paul said.

Jimmie's face brightened. He looked at Johnny, Alan, and the faces of the other players standing around. His expression clearly said, "I told you so, didn't I?"

He felt good. Everything was settled now.

He was going to pitch. All winter long he'd been thinking about it, while he read a book on big-league pitchers. He used to think a pitcher had to be tall and able to throw a ball faster than anyone else on the team. But that wasn't so. The book had told about pitchers who weren't very tall and were still great hurlers. It had told about pitchers who weren't the fastest throwers on their teams, but were smart and could throw hooks that struck men out like anything.

That was the kind of pitcher he wanted to be. Smart, and throw a lot of hooks. Jimmie smiled happily. He looked at Ervie, who was standing beside him with his hands in his pockets. But he couldn't tell whether Ervie was happy or not.

Something about him made Jimmie lose his smile. Something about the way Ervie was looking at Paul Karoski.

2

Jimmie took a deep breath. He turned away from Ervie and tried not to be bothered by him. He wished he could leave Ervie home. Then he wouldn't be afraid to tell the boys anything. With Ervie around, he had to be careful what he said and what he did.

His eyes roved over the faces again. They settled on a boy a little taller and fatter than Ervie. His face was moon-shaped. His nose was like an old-fashioned shoe button.

"Hey, Tiny! Are you going to catch for us this year?"

Tiny Zimmer shook his head. "No. I'm going to play with the Red Rockets."

"The Red Rockets?" Jimmie's forehead knotted into a frown. "Why? Don't you want to play with us?"

Tiny shrugged. "They asked me last week. They've already given me a jersey."

"Well, how do you like that?" Jimmie said, disgusted. "What are you doing here if you're playing with the Red Rockets?"

Tiny shrugged again. "I came with Paul."

Jimmie glared at him. Tiny wasn't a good player, but he had nerve to stand behind the plate. Jimmie couldn't think of anybody else to take Tiny's place. Nobody had ever asked for the position. It was a tough one to play. Besides, Tiny was the only boy who owned a catcher's mitt.

Jimmie kicked the short-cropped grass with the toe of his sneaker. "A fine start this is! How are we going to play in the Grasshoppers League if we don't have a catcher?"

The Grasshoppers League was starting soon. In order to join, a team had to have at least nine players. Their names had to be in on a certain date. If the names weren't in, the team's chance to enter was lost.

Jimmie wet his lips. He looked at Ervie. If only Ervie was four or five years older, he thought, then he could catch.

"Well, are we going to have a team in the league, or not?" Jimmie snapped. "We need a catcher. Who's going to catch?"

"I'll catch," a soft, deep voice spoke up from the rear of the group.

Jimmie rose on his toes. "Mose Solomon? Do you own a catcher's mask and a mitt, Mose?"

"My big brother does. But he'll let me take them. He bought a new outfit."

Jimmie breathed a sigh of relief. "Will you go after them, Mose? Then we can play a game."

"Okay!" Mose ran off.

Most of the kids had their gloves with them. So did Jimmie. He had also brought a ball and bat, hoping there would be enough players to choose up sides.

"What are we calling our team?" Wishy Walters asked. "The Planets?"

"Sure. The same as last year," Jimmie said. He was anxious to play ball. He wanted to get on the mound and pitch. He wanted to prove to those boys who wouldn't believe he could pitch that he was as good as Paul Karoski — or even better. "Let's choose up sides!" he said.

Johnny Lukon chose with him. Jimmie tossed his bat to Johnny, who caught it near

9

the middle. Then, hand over hand, the two boys worked to the top of the handle. Johnny won first choice.

"Paul," he said.

"Mose," Jimmie said.

The two teams were picked at last. There weren't enough players, so Jimmie asked Ervie if he'd like to play.

"Sure," said Ervie.

"Okay. You play right field." Jimmie pointed to where he meant.

"I know," murmured Ervie quietly.

Jimmie and Johnny chose for last raps. Jimmie won. Mose Solomon arrived with a mask and catcher's mitt. The batting cage was pulled out of the way and the game began. Jimmie was glad Mose was catching. It would be almost like a real game.

The leadoff hitter stepped to the plate.

Jimmie put his right foot on the rubber and wound up. He threw one fast toward the plate. It was a foot outside. The batter let it go.

"Put it over!" somebody yelled.

He threw another wild pitch. Then one was close to the inside corner, but the batter didn't swing at it.

"What're you waiting for?" Jimmie cried.

"Put 'em over the plate!" Johnny Lukon wailed.

He was ready to pitch when Wishy said, "Jimmie! Here comes Mr. Nichols! Ask him to umpire."

"Good idea! Mr. Nichols!" Jimmie shouted across the field. "Oh, Mr. Nichols! Will you umpire for us?"

Mr. Nichols was a tall, dark-haired man with a quick, happy smile. He often came to the park to watch the kids play.

He waved a greeting. "Sure, Jimmie," he said. "I'll be glad to."

He stepped behind the pitcher's mound and the game resumed.

Jimmie pitched.

"Ball one!" said Mr. Nichols.

Jimmie pitched again.

"Ball two!" said Mr. Nichols.

Jimmie grew worried. Why couldn't he throw that ball over the plate? The home base looked like a big, flat dish up there. It should be easy to throw the ball over.

But Jimmie walked that man, and he walked the next.

"Take it easy," Mr. Nichols advised him. "Don't throw so hard."

Maybe that was the trouble, Jimmie thought. He threw easier. *Smack!* The ball sailed over second base! A run scored. The runner on first stopped on third. The hitter stopped on second. A two-bagger!

Jimmie's heart sank. This wasn't the way it should be. He had plenty of speed. He had a hook. Those batters weren't supposed to hit his pitches.

At last Johnny's team made three outs. The score was 4 to 0, and the first inning was only half over!

Jimmie's side scored two runs.

The second inning was a repetition of the first. Johnny's team was knocking Jimmie's pitches all over the lot. Before three outs were made, four more runs had been scored.

Jimmie came to bat. He stepped into one of Paul's fast balls for a line drive over short. The ball sailed deep into the outfield. Jimmie raced around the bases and stopped on third. A smile tugged at the corners of his mouth. That hit had felt good and solid. It made up a little for those bad throws and the men he had walked.

Someday he would be a good pitcher, he thought. He'd throw the ball wherever he wanted to. High, low, inside — anywhere. All he needed was practice.

3

"Mr. Nichols," Johnny Lukon said, "we want to play in the Grasshoppers League, but we need a manager. Would you be our manager, Mr. Nichols?"

Mr. Nichols smiled. His gray eyes twinkled as if he had just been honored by something very important.

"You sure you want me to be your manager?" he asked.

"Yes. We talked about it. Would you manage us, please, Mr. Nichols?"

Mr. Nichols chuckled. "Okay. I'd be glad

to. I know most of the boys who run the Grasshoppers League, and we will get our team entered as soon as possible."

He looked at the hot, anxious faces around him. "Now, do you have a captain?"

Jimmie stepped forward. "I'm the captain," he said.

"Okay. Suppose you come to my house tonight, Jimmie, and give me the names of your players so that I'll know who's on our team?"

"Yes, sir."

"What about bats and gloves? Does everybody have them?"

"Most of us have."

"What about balls?" Billy Hutt asked. "Those are furnished by the league," Mr. Nichols said. He glanced at the mask and mitt in Mose Solomon's hands. "Are those yours, Mose?"

"Yes."

"Good. Can you boys be here again the same time tomorrow? We'll go through fielding and batting practices."

"Sure!" the boys said happily.

Jimmie felt a tug at his sleeve. He turned.

"I want to go home," Ervie said.

"Oh, please, Ervie," said Jimmie. "Not yet. We have plenty of time."

"I'm hungry," Ervie said.

"Hungry? Is that all you want to do? Eat?"

Ervie blinked his eyes. "I think we should go home. It's late."

"You go home if you want to," Jimmie replied gruffly. "I'm staying here."

Ervie peered up at him. There was hurt in his eyes. Jimmie turned his back to him, hoping Ervie would go home. But when he looked around, Ervie was still there, gazing at him with those haunting blue eyes.

"Look, Ervie," he pleaded, "I'm captain of the Planets. I'm supposed to stay here. I can't go before the others go. Can't you understand?"

Ervie didn't answer. He just blinked his eyes again.

"Listen, Ervie," Jimmie said in a low voice, "I want to practice pitching. The best place is here on the diamond. I need the practice. You want us to be ready when the league starts, don't you? You want us to have a good team, don't you?"

"Yes," said Ervie.

"Then will you stay awhile longer?"

"No," said Ervie. "I want to go home. I'm hungry."

4

Jimmie walked ahead of Ervie. He didn't look back once until he reached the corner. Ervie was about twenty feet behind him.

"You walk too fast," said Ervie, puffing.

When they reached the corner, Jimmie took Ervie's hand. He felt bad because he had been mean to Ervie. "Maybe you're right, Ervie," he said. "Maybe it is late. Come on."

They entered the kitchen. Jimmie smelled the cooked potatoes and ham, and his mouth watered. His stomach felt empty now, too.

Mrs. Todd turned from the kitchen stove. Her shiny black hair hung in soft waves. She was wearing a blue shirt with white polka dots.

"Well," she said, "look what the wind blew in. My two baseball players!" A smile flickered in her eyes. "It seems, though, that someone's memory isn't as good now that baseball season is here."

Jimmie was puzzled. "What do you mean, Mom?"

She pointed at the clock on the wall. "Do you see what time it is?"

Jimmie looked. "It's five minutes to five."

"Yes. Can you remember what time I asked you boys to come home?"

"Four o'clock. But nobody had a watch, Mom," Jimmie added hastily.

His eyes met Ervie's, and his face turned red. He had lied again. He had not wanted to come home. He had wanted to stay. If Ervie hadn't insisted on coming home, he would have been at the field yet.

He prayed Ervie wouldn't tell on him. Ervie didn't.

Mrs. Todd ruffled Jimmie's hair. "Well, I suppose that none of you baseball players would carry a watch with you. Daddy is home and supper is about ready. Wash your hands, while I set the table."

After supper Jimmie asked his mother if he could go to Paul Karoski's house. She consented.

Paul was in the backyard, playing pitch and catch with someone. When Jimmie reached the corner of the house, he saw that the other boy was Tiny Zimmer.

"Hi," Jimmie called.

"Hi," Tiny said. He was crouched behind a piece of wood that was supposed to be home plate. He took one glance at Jimmie, then turned his attention back to Paul.

Paul didn't say anything. He was too interested in winding up and keeping his eyes on the target that Tiny had made with his glove. Paul's left hand went back over his shoulder, then came around fast. The ball snapped from his fingers and sped toward the mitt. *Plop!*

"Thataboy, Paul," Tiny said. "Right over the outside corner."

Jimmie watched Paul throw awhile. But Paul didn't look at him once, as if he weren't even there.

Paul looked pretty good, Jimmie thought. But he should play first base, or the outfield. The Planets didn't need two pitchers. Jimmie would be the only one they needed.

Wishy Walters came up behind Jimmie. He watched for a while too, then said, "Want to come to my house, Jimmie? I have a hard rubber ball. We can play a few games."

"I might as well," said Jimmie.

Wishy's house was a block down the street. It was made of brick with a wide porch in front. Mr. and Mrs. Walters were sitting on the porch. Jimmie spoke to them. They asked how his mother and father were. Then Wishy got his rubber ball.

"I'll be Cleveland," Wishy said.

"I'll be Detroit," Jimmie said.

They went to the side of the house, then threw fingers to see who would "bat" first. Wishy won. He stood close to the house and Jimmie about six feet behind him. Wishy would throw the ball against the house. When it bounced back, Jimmie would try to catch it. If he caught it, it would mean an out. If he missed it, it would mean an error and a "man" would get on first base. If the ball went past him and he didn't touch it, it would mean a hit.

Wishy was ahead 10 to 6 by the third inning. Jimmie didn't care. He wasn't interested in the game, now. He was thinking about Paul. Paul was his best friend, yet Paul had hardly looked at him when he was there a while ago.

Was Paul mad at him? Was he annoyed because Jimmie wanted to pitch? But he did say he'd play the outfield, didn't he? Didn't he mean it? Did he still want to pitch?

But I want to pitch, Jimmie told himself. We're only going to play one game a week. There won't be enough games for two pitchers. Can't Paul understand that?

There were footsteps behind him. Jimmie

turned. Tiny Zimmer was coming down the cemented alleyway, a big grin on his moon-shaped face.

"Hi, fellas," he said.

"Hi, Tiny," Jimmie murmured. "Where's Paul?"

"Home." The grin on Tiny's face widened. "I have some news for you guys. Paul isn't going to play with the Planets. He's going to play with us. The Red Rockets."

5

Jimmie went home. He kicked a stone in the driveway. He banged the toe of his shoe against the first step that led to the porch. Why did Paul have to play with the Red Rockets? Why?

He went inside. His mother was in the kitchen, mending a pair of Ervie's pants.

"What's the matter, Jimmie?" she asked.

"Nothing," said Jimmie. He went into the living room. Ervie was playing with his toy stagecoach on the thick rug.

"Hi, Jimmie," he said. "Will you play with me?"

"Not now."

Jimmie turned away and headed for his room. He could feel Ervie's eyes on his back.

He sat on his bed and thought about Paul Karoski. Paul and he were such great buddies. They were like brothers. They had always played together, ever since they were old enough to walk. Sure, they would get mad at each other once in a while. Who didn't? But it never lasted long.

How could Paul do that? Jimmie thought. How could Paul turn his back on him, and on the Planets, to play on another team?

Jimmie swallowed an ache in his throat and wiped his eyes.

"What's wrong, Jimmie?" a voice said softly behind him.

Ervie had come in so quietly Jimmie had not heard him.

"Nothing," he said. He went to his desk

and yanked out a drawer. He took out two sheets of heavy yellow paper and a box of crayons.

He tried to think of something to draw. But his mind was filled with thoughts of Paul. Without Paul the Planets would not amount to anything. He could hit. He could run. And if anything ever happened to Jimmie, he could pitch.

Well, thought Jimmie angrily, let him pitch for the Red Rockets! I don't care!

He pulled the drawer out again and shoved the paper and box of crayons back into it. Then he rose and put an arm around Ervie's shoulder.

"Come on, Ervie," he said. "I'll play with you."

6

The Planets couldn't practice the next afternoon. It rained off and on and the field was too wet. Thursday morning though, the sun came out nice and bright. By afternoon the field was dry.

The team gathered at the field. They played catch for a while. Some of the boys talked about Paul.

"Why did he quit?" one of them asked.

"I don't know."

"He's going to pitch for the Red Rockets, that's why."

"The Red Rockets? He belongs to us, doesn't he?"

"He doesn't have to. He can belong to any team he wants to."

Jimmie pretended he didn't hear them. He wished that they would stop talking about Paul. After all, he was their pitcher. Once he got going, he'd be even better than Paul. Just wait and see.

Mr. Nichols arrived. He was wearing a blue baseball cap and a sweatshirt. He looked like a real manager now.

"Hi, boys!" His gray eyes sparkled as he looked at the faces. "Where's Paul Karoski?" he asked.

"He joined the Red Rockets," Wishy said. "We're going to miss him. He was a good player."

"He was the best pitcher we had," Johnny Lukon said.

"We don't need a good pitcher," Wishy said. "Jimmie can pitch as well as anybody. What we need are hitters." Jimmie looked at Wishy and felt a little better that somebody was on his side.

"Well, Jimmie Todd can be our pitcher," Mr. Nichols said. "I think that after some practice he'll be just as good as Paul Karoski. Let's hope he'll be better!"

Some of the boys laughed. Jimmie felt like smiling himself.

Yet he wished that Paul was playing with them. It wasn't right that Paul should play with another team. He belonged here — with the Planets.

"Let's have batting practice," Mr. Nichols suggested. "Jimmie, take these three balls and get on the mound. Some of you boys pull that batting cage closer to the plate."

The cage was moved up.

"Johnny, Alan, and Billy," Mr. Nichols said, "you three can start to bat. Hit five and lay one down. Okay, Jimmie! Throw 'em in there!"

Jimmie stood on the rubber, made his windup, and threw the ball. Mr. Nichols, standing behind the batting cage, watched him. The pitch was wide. Johnny let it go by.

"Outside!" Mr. Nichols said.

Jimmie picked up another ball, wound up, and threw.

"Too high!" Mr. Nichols said.

The next pitch hit the dirt in front of the plate.

The manager gathered up the three balls and tossed them back to Jimmie. "Come on, Jimmie, boy. Take your time. Get 'em over."

Jimmie was careful with the next pitch. He didn't throw it hard. It went over the plate. Johnny swung at it and the ball sailed out to left field. The next pitch was low, but it came in easy, and Johnny swung again. He missed. "Come on! Throw 'em in here, will you?" Johnny cried.

"I wish Paul was pitching for us," Alan Warzcak murmured softly, but loud enough for Jimmie to hear. "He puts 'em all over."

"I know," Billy Hutt said. "We used to have fine batting practice when he was pitching!"

"All right, boys. Enough of that," Mr. Nichols cautioned. "Come on, Jimmie. Take your time, boy. You'll get 'em in there."

But Jimmie couldn't get them in there. After a while, Mr. Nichols went out to the mound himself and pitched.

7

They practiced all the next week. First they had batting practice, then Mr. Nichols would hit balls to the infielders and outfielders. While Mr. Nichols did that, Jimmie practiced pitching.

He had learned to throw a drop. He was proud of it. Now, if he could only get his fast throws over the plate . . .

At the Friday afternoon practice Mr. Nichols called the boys together.

"I've scheduled a game with the Pirates for tomorrow afternoon," he said. "Everybody be here at one-thirty. I'll try to get a couple more games before the league starts so that we won't plunge into it cold."

Jimmie was up bright and early Saturday morning. After breakfast he went to Mose Solomon's house. Mose's mother came to the door and said that Mose was still in bed.

"Who's that, Ma?" Mose's voice came from somewhere upstairs.

"Jimmie Todd!" she called back. She smiled at Jimmie. "I guess he wasn't asleep. Just lying there. You want to come in and wait for him?"

"Thank you," said Jimmie.

After Mose washed, dressed, and ate his breakfast, he brought his mitt and played catch with Jimmie.

"Give me a target," Jimmie said.

Mose held his mitt in front of his left shoulder until Jimmie could put a ball in that spot. Then he'd change it to his right shoulder and then in front of his chest. The ball seemed to go everywhere but where Mose held the mitt.

"Come on, Jimmie. Come on," Mose said encouragingly.

"I'm trying!" cried Jimmie.

After a while he became tired. "Let's quit," he said. "I've still got to pitch this afternoon."

As the hour of the game drew near, Jimmie's stomach tightened into knots. He wanted so much to be a pitcher, but he wasn't doing too well. If he only had control . . .

He walked a man in the first inning. The next man singled, sending the runner to third. Jimmie stood on the rubber and looked at the two fingers Mose held below his mitt. Mose was signaling for a curve ball.

Jimmie's hands trembled. No one was out, and already two men were on. One was in scoring position. Everybody was looking at Jimmie. They were waiting to see what he could do.

"He'll walk you!" a voice shouted from the grandstand. "Just stand there with your bat on your shoulder, Mike!"

His heart thumped in his chest. Perspiration covered his face. There seemed to be too much going on. People were shouting. . . . Mose was giving him a target. . . . The infielders were talking it up. . . . Two men were on bases. . . . He tried to think about everything at once.

He wound up. The runner on third took a big lead. Jimmie stopped his windup, whipped the ball to third. The boy ran back. Alan Warzcak tagged him before his foot touched the bag.

"Balk!" shouted the umpire, who stood behind Jimmie.

Jimmie was startled. He looked at Mr. Nichols, sitting in the dugout. Mr. Nichols nodded.

"You can't throw a ball to a base once you've started to wind up," the umpire said. "Never wind up with men on base. They can steal on you. Okay, kid!" he said to the runner on third. "Take the base!" He turned to the runner on first. "Go to second!"

Mr. Nichols trotted out to the mound. He put an arm around Jimmie's shoulder. "You're all nerved up, Jimmie. Relax. Take it easy. This is just a scrub game. About that windup and throw when a runner's on base — do you understand it now?"

"Yes," Jimmie murmured.

"Okay." Mr. Nichols patted him on the shoulder and grinned. "Just let 'em hit it."

The Pirates scored three runs in the first inning. The Planets tied it in the second. The third inning went by scoreless. In the fourth Jimmie walked two men in a row, and the next man hit a homer that put the Pirates way ahead again. The Pirates made two more runs in the fifth, and there the game ended. Score — 8 to 3.

"Don't worry," Mr. Nichols said as the boys gathered their bats and gloves and headed sadly for home. "We have a good team. Once Jimmie finds that plate, nobody will beat us."

Jimmie kept his eyes straight ahead. I'll find it, he thought. I have to find it, or we might as well not join the league.

8

The Planets played a game Tuesday afternoon against the Mohawks. Jimmie felt a little more confident before the game began. He had practiced a lot. His control was improving. Mr. Nichols said so himself.

The first two innings went by without a man reaching first base. Lou Rodell, the Planets' shortstop, hit a grounder to short in the top of the third inning. The Mohawks' shortstop caught it and threw it over the first baseman's head. Lou ran to second on the play.

Jimmie stepped to the plate. He batted fifth in the batting order. He pulled his helmet down tight on his head, gripped his bat near the end of the handle, and dug his toes into the dirt.

The ball came in. It was low. Jimmie let it go by.

"Ball!" cried the umpire.

The catcher threw the ball back to the pitcher. Jimmie waited again. The pitcher stretched his hands high, brought them down. He looked over his shoulder at the runner on second, then threw the ball toward the plate.

It came in chest-high. It looked like a strike. Jimmie stepped into it. He swung. *Crack!* The ball sailed toward left center field. Lou scored. Jimmie rounded second, then third.

"Go! Go!" yelled Mr. Nichols, who was coaching third.

Jimmie ran like a deer. He crossed the plate for a home run!

"Thataboy, Jimmie!" Wishy Walters shouted. "Win your own ball game!"

The homer made Jimmie feel good. They were ahead now — 2 to 0. If they could just hold that lead . . .

Kippy Lake flied out to center. Wishy struck out. George Bardino popped a fly to the pitcher. Three outs in six pitched balls. Boy, that was quick, thought Jimmie.

The Planets ran out onto the field.

Jimmie pitched. "Ball!" said the umpire.

"Ball two!"

"Strike!"

"Ball three!"

"Ball four! Take your base!"

Jimmie trembled. He couldn't walk any more men. He couldn't. . . .

He stretched, pitched. The batter held

out his bat. He bunted the ball down the third base line. Jimmie raced after it. He picked it up, made a motion to throw to second. Too late there! He heaved it to first.

"Out!" yelled the base umpire.

But throwing out the man didn't help Jimmie's control. He became wilder and wilder. He walked in runs. When he came to bat, he didn't feel like hitting. He wished the ball game was over. He wished they would call it off.

Mr. Nichols talked with the Mohawks' manager during the fourth inning. Then he came to the dugout and said:

"This is the last inning, boys. At the rate we're going, we'll be playing all day."

The Mohawks won, 14 to 4.

Jimmie walked home with Ervie. The rest of the team paired off by themselves.

"You lost, didn't you?" Ervie said.

"Yes," said Jimmie. "The Mohawks swamped us. But we'll win the next one," he added quickly. "You wait and see."

He thought of Paul Karoski. If Paul played with the Planets, things would be different. He'd feel more like playing if Paul was on the team.

He missed Paul a lot. He missed Paul's nice, quiet manners. He missed Paul's coming over to watch television with him. Paul used to come almost every day, and Jimmie would go to visit him, too. Even Mrs. Todd missed him. Every once in a while she asked about him.

"Do you think the Planets are good enough to play in the Grasshoppers League, Jimmie?" Ervie asked in his easy, quiet way.

Jimmie looked at him, startled. "Why? Don't you think so, Ervie?"

Ervie was younger than he. He couldn't

know very much about it. But deep in his heart Jimmie knew that whatever Ervie said meant a lot to him.

"No," Ervie replied. "I don't. The Planets aren't going to win any games. They don't have a good — I mean —" Ervie paused.

"They don't have a good what, Ervie?" Jimmie said, and held his breath.

Ervie's eyes met his squarely. "They don't have a good pitcher, that's why!"

9

The following Friday, at the supper table, Mr. Todd said, "I'm going fishing in the morning. How'd you like to come along, Jimmie?"

Jimmie's heart leaped. "Sure! Where are we going, Dad?"

"To Spring Lake. The boys at the shop say the pikes are really biting."

Jimmie clapped his hands. "Oh, boy! We haven't fished in weeks, have we, Dad?"

"Last time was about a month ago," Mr. Todd said with a smile.

They were up at five o'clock the next morning. Mrs. Todd made a basket of sandwiches, a quart thermos of coffee for Dad, and a pint thermos of milk for Jimmie.

"Why don't you come along, Mom?" Jimmie asked.

"What — and leave Ervie home?" She smiled and pulled his ear. "No, never mind. We'll plan a picnic soon for the whole family. I'm not much of a fisherman, anyway."

Mr. Todd rented a boat at a place called Kam's Boat Landing. The boat was equipped with a motor. He and Jimmie put their fishing gear into the boat and chugged out to where the lake was smooth as glass and deep.

They baited their hooks with minnows that Mr. Todd had bought at the landing. Jimmie baited his own hook. His father had

47

taught him how to do it. Then they cast their lines into the water and sat there and waited for the fish to bite.

Seagulls flew in the still air around them. A crow cawed in the distance. Once in a while the sun peeked through a crack in the gray clouds.

Jimmie grew restless. They had sat here all morning and they hadn't caught a fish yet.

"What happened to all the fish those men were talking about, Dad?" he asked.

His father grinned. "I don't know. They must have seen us coming and swum off. What's the matter? Getting tired?"

"Well — kind of."

"Have a sandwich," his father suggested.

Jimmie took a sandwich out of the basket and poured himself a glass of milk. He liked this part of it. It was fun to eat out here in the boat. His father ate too, but steadily watched his line.

Another half hour dragged by.

Jimmie straightened his back, stretched his arms, and yawned. "We're not going to catch any fish, Dad," he said. "Let's go home."

"Now, hold your horses," said Mr. Todd. "We're not going home yet. Let's try another spot."

They tried another spot. It didn't seem any better.

"I'm getting tired, Dad," Jimmie murmured.

"Yes, I know. And impatient, too."

Just then the red and white bobber on Jimmie's line plunged down into the water! Jimmie gripped the rod.

"I caught one, Dad! I caught one!" he cried excitedly.

He wound the reel and felt the fish fight on the end of the line. He wondered what it was. It felt like a big one.

Finally, a long wriggling fish leaped from the water.

"A pike!" Mr. Todd shouted. "And a beauty, at that!"

Mr. Todd grabbed the leader, removed the pike from the hook, and dropped it, still wriggling, into the creel.

"See?" he said. "Isn't this catch worth all that time you spent waiting?"

Jimmie's heart throbbed. He grinned happily. "It sure is!" he said.

"Patience," Mr. Todd said. "It's an important thing in fishing. It's the same in baseball or anything else. When you want something, you have to keep at it. But you can't be in a hurry. Suppose I had become discouraged earlier the way you did and wanted to quit?

We would've gone home with nothing. That would be a fine way to greet Mom, wouldn't it?"

Jimmie smiled. "I guess you're right, Dad," he said.

10

They had fish for supper. Mr. Todd had caught two, right after Jimmie had caught his, so there was plenty to go around.

Early in the evening Jimmie began to think about Paul again. Lots of times on Saturday nights Paul would come and watch television with him. Sometimes his mother and father would come, too. Now it was more than two weeks since Paul had been here.

It was Tiny Zimmer's fault, Jimmie told

himself. Tiny was the one who had asked Paul to play with the Red Rockets.

Suddenly, Jimmie had an idea. Maybe if Mr. and Mrs. Karoski came, Paul would come, too!

He went to his mother.

"Mom, why don't you invite Mr. and Mrs. Karoski over? It's Saturday night, and they haven't been over in a long time."

"I thought about that, too." His mother smiled. "I'll call them right now."

The telephone was in the living room. She dialed a number.

"Hello? Josie? This is Lynn. How are you?"

They talked a bit. Finally Mrs. Todd invited Mrs. Karoski and her husband over for the evening.

"Tell them to bring Paul, too!" Jimmie whispered.

"Bring Paul with you," Mrs. Todd said.

She hung up, smiling. "They'll be glad to come!" she said.

Forty-five minutes later Mr. and Mrs. Karoski came. But Paul wasn't with them.

"Where's Paul?" Jimmie asked Mr. Karoski.

Mr. Karoski was a middle-aged man with a mustache and horn-rimmed glasses. He shrugged his shoulders. "He's home. He didn't want to come."

"Why not?"

Mrs. Karoski answered. "I don't know. He just didn't want to come. I don't understand that boy. Sometimes he won't say anything."

"I know why," a small voice said.

Jimmie looked at Ervie. Something that felt like wire clamped around his chest.

Ervie looked up at Mrs. Karoski. His blue

eyes seemed bigger than ever. "He's mad at Jimmie," he said. "Paul wants to pitch, and Jimmie wants to pitch. They both want to pitch for the Planets."

Jimmie bit his lip. His face flushed.

"Thanks a lot, Ervie!" he cried loudly, and ran out of the room.

11

The whole Todd family went to church Sunday morning. Afterward, Mrs. Todd cooked steak, mashed potatoes, carrots, peas, and corn. She cooked onions with the steak, too, but neither Jimmie nor Ervie liked onions.

Jimmie helped his mother with the dishes. Then the family drove to the park.

It was a nice day. The golden sun splashed its warmth over the green grass, trees, and everywhere. The park was crowded with families. Children laughed. Mothers wheeled baby carriages.

Mr. Todd parked the car. Everybody piled out. They walked on the grass that felt like a carpet under their feet. They stopped and talked with friends.

Then they walked up a small hill. Here and there rosebushes and geraniums decorated the park. Chestnut trees loomed into the sky. Gray squirrels jerked their tails as they hopped over the grass.

"Look, Mom!" Ervie cried. "Squirrels!"

Cries and yells echoed from beyond the hill.

"Sounds like a baseball game," Mr. Todd said.

They reached the top of the hill. A ball game was going on in the field beyond.

Jimmie saw that boys of his own age were playing. He recognized some of the boys from his team. Then he saw who was pitching, and he stopped in his tracks and shoved his hands hard into his pockets.

"What do you want to watch that game for? It's just a scrub game," he said.

"Paul Karoski is pitching," Mr. Todd said. "Let's just watch a few minutes."

They went closer to the field. They stopped beside other people who were watching. Jimmie remained behind. He didn't want any of the boys to see him. They might ask him to play, and he didn't want to. Not with Paul there. Paul was annoyed at him. He'd probably quit if Jimmie played.

Paul went through his windup. His left arm went back. His right leg lifted. Then his arm came around and the ball snapped from his fingers. It sped toward the plate like a bullet. The batter swung.

"Strike three!" the umpire shouted.

Mr. Todd chuckled. "Say! Paul looks good, doesn't he? He has beautiful form for a kid. That boy will make a great pitcher some-day."

The words stung Jimmie. They hurt more because his father had said them.

"One of these days I'll be as good as he is," he said stiffly. "I can throw faster than he can now. All I need is control."

His father looked at him. "Oh? You told me you were pitching, but you didn't tell me you were that good."

Jimmie's face colored. "Well, that's what Mr. Nichols said."

He met Ervie's eyes. His face grew hot and sweat shone on his forehead. He had said the wrong thing again. He could tell by the look Ervie gave him.

"Let's go," he said. "I'm getting tired standing here."

His father patted him on the shoulder. "Okay, Jimmie. We'll go."

12

On Monday morning Jimmie sat on the steps of the back porch. He was alone. Ervie was somewhere in the house, playing by himself.

Jimmie had never been so unhappy in all his life. Just because he wanted to pitch, he thought. What was so wonderful about pitching, anyway?

If he had let Paul pitch for the Planets, everything would be all right. They would have a good team, and he and Paul would still be pals.

At last he went into the house and brought out a tennis ball. He stood in the driveway, threw the ball against the wall of his house, and caught it on a bounce. He did this for a while, then he yelled for Ervie.

"Ervie! Will you come out?"

A few minutes later Ervie came out of the house. "Did you want me, Jimmie?"

"Yes. Will you get my bat and hit some grounders to me?"

"Sure!" Ervie said, and scampered back into the house. He came out with Jimmie's yellow bat. Jimmie handed him the tennis ball.

"You stay here," he advised Ervie. "I'll get down by the fence. Just hit 'em on the ground."

Jimmie trotted to the fence at the edge of the lawn. Ervie tossed the ball up with his left hand, then tried to hit it with the bat.

The ball dropped to the ground before he could swing the bat around. "Come on, Ervie! You can hit it! It's easy!"

Ervie tried again. The same thing happened. At last he did hit it, but the ball dribbled so slowly that it stopped before it was halfway to Jimmie.

Jimmie shook his head.

A boy walked by the end of the driveway. Jimmie caught a glimpse of him before he got behind the next building.

"Wishy!" he shouted. "Wishy Walters!"

Wishy poked his head around the corner and waved. "Hi, Jimmie!"

"Come here!" Jimmie motioned.

Wishy came forward. His heels clicked on the cement driveway.

"Would you like to hit me some grounders?" asked Jimmie.

"Grounders?" Wishy's forehead puckered

in a frown. "You're a pitcher. Why do you want me to hit you grounders?"

Jimmie thought a moment. He didn't know whether to tell Wishy. But Wishy was a good friend. He could trust Wishy with a secret.

"If I can get Paul back on the Planets, I'll play an infield position," Jimmie said. "I don't think I'll ever be a pitcher, Wishy."

"Oh, sure, you will," said Wishy. "All you need is control. You have a lot of speed, Jimmie."

"But time is going fast, Wishy. The day when we play our first league game will be here before we know it. And we're not ready. We've lost every practice game we've played."

"But we've only played two," argued Wishy. "Anyway, Paul won't play with us now. He's going to stick with the Red Rockets."

Jimmie paled. "How do you know?"

"He told me," said Wishy. "And when Paul says something, he means it."

Jimmie stared at the ground. "But — he was my best friend. He'll play with us if I tell him he can pitch. I'm sure he will." The thought of it excited him. "Come on, Wishy. Hit me grounders!"

"Okay," said Wishy. "If you want me to."

Wishy tossed the ball up just as Ervie had. But he hit it. Jimmie caught the ball on a hop. He threw it back to Wishy, who caught it, and hit it back to him. At first he hit it easy, then harder. The tennis ball would bounce across the lawn like a wild rabbit. Sometimes Jimmie missed it. But most of the time he caught it.

He began to like it.

"Wait!" he said. "I'll get my baseball and glove!"

This was more like the real thing. A couple of times Wishy hit the ball over the fence and Jimmie sent Ervie after it.

Finally Jimmie had to sit down.

"Boy, I'm tired!" he said. He sprawled out on the lawn. His chest heaved.

When he caught his breath he sat up. "Will you come over after supper, Wishy?"

Wishy nodded. "Sure."

"Thataboy!" said Jimmie.

The Planets had batting practice that afternoon. Jimmie pitched to four men. He didn't do any better than he had before, so Mr. Nichols asked Johnny Lukon to pitch to the batters. Johnny was good at it. A lot better than Jimmie.

"I don't know what I'm going to do with you," Mr. Nichols said as Jimmie waited for his turn to bat. "I thought your control was improving, but I guess it isn't. You have speed, and a nice curve. If you had control, you'd be the best pitcher in the league."

Jimmie didn't say anything. What Mr.

Nichols had just told him didn't make him feel bad. He wasn't worried, or hurt.

His turn to bat came. He swung at the first four pitches without missing. The fifth throw was high and he missed it by a mile. He knew he shouldn't have swung at it. But he felt as if he could hit anything today.

After the boys hit, Mr. Nichols had the infielders practice. Jimmie sat on the bench and watched them. He knew the routine. The third baseman would catch the ball and throw it to first. The first baseman would throw it home. Home to third again, and back around the horn.

He watched Lou Rodell at short. Lou seemed to be afraid of grounders. He would back up a lot. Jimmie noticed that Mr. Nichols didn't hit the ball too hard to him.

After infield practice was over, Mr. Nichols called the boys together.

"I've arranged another game with the Pirates," he said. "They didn't beat us as bad as the Mohawks did. The game will be played here tomorrow afternoon at two o'clock. Tell your folks to come if they'd like to."

Jimmie didn't tell his mother and father about the game. He didn't want them to see him pitch. Anyway, his father couldn't go. He had to work. Jimmie was glad of that.

The game began. This time the Pirates had last raps. Johnny Lukon led off with a single. Alan flied out. Then Billy Hutt hit a grounder past third for a two-bagger. Johnny stopped on third as the fielder threw in to cover home.

Lou grounded through second, scoring Johnny and Billy. Jimmie came to bat. He let a knee-high pitch go by.

"Strike one!" said the umpire.

The next two pitches were balls. Then another strike.

Jimmie pulled his helmet down tight,

braced his feet in the dirt, and waited for the next pitch. The ball sped in, chest-high and over the heart of the plate.

Jimmie blasted it. It sailed high into center field. The fielder ran back, caught it, and threw it in!

"Get back! Get back!" yelled the coach on first to Lou.

The Pirates' second baseman caught the throw-in from center field and snapped the ball to first. It reached there before Lou could tag up.

"Out!" shouted the umpire.

Three outs. The Planets took the field.

The first batter grounded out to third. The ball was hit solid. That was just luck he hit straight at Alan, Jimmie thought. Jimmie would have walked the next hitter, but the batter swung at bad throws and struck out. The third man flied out to center.

"Nice going, Jimmie!" Lou yelled.

"Nice pitching, Jimmie!" Alan said.

After that things weren't so good. Jimmie walked a man in the second inning, and in the third he hit a man on the shoulder. He began to worry. The Pirates started to hit him hard. When they didn't hit, Jimmie helped them by walking their men.

In the fourth, Mr. Nichols went out to the mound. He called Johnny from first.

"I think Jimmie is wild because he's worried he might hit another batter," Mr. Nichols said. "You two boys switch positions for the next two innings. We're only playing five. Okay?"

"Okay," Jimmie said.

He didn't care. Matter of fact, he was glad.

He liked first base. He moved into position and mixed his cries with the other infielders'.

"Come on, Paul!" he shouted. "Come on, P—!"

His throat caught. He looked around hurriedly. He hoped nobody had heard him yell Paul's name instead of Johnny's.

14

During practice the next day, Jimmie went up to the manager. "Are all the names of our players in yet, Mr. Nichols?" he asked.

"Not yet. I'll have to have them in before Thursday."

"Thursday?" Jimmie's brows puckered. "Is that when we play our first Grasshoppers League game?"

Mr. Nichols nodded. "That's right! Better work hard on your control, Jimmie. Winning that first game is important!"

"I know," murmured Jimmie.

After practice, Jimmie didn't go home

with the others. He asked Wishy Walters to stay with him.

"I want you to hit me some grounders, Wishy," he said. "Will you?"

"Sure," said Wishy.

"Hit 'em hard as you can!" Jimmie said, and ran out to shortstop position.

Wishy hit five grounders to him. Jimmie caught them all. Then Mr. Nichols, who had been watching, picked up Wishy's glove and went to first base. He watched Jimmie run behind the grounders and catch them as if it was easy. Jimmie saw Mr. Nichols on first and pegged the balls to him. His throws were good. They seldom were directly over the bag, but they were close enough. Once in a while he made Mr. Nichols stretch for one, but not often.

Finally, Mr. Nichols exclaimed, "Say! You look sharp out there! How long have you been playing infield?"

"I played infield last year," Jimmie said. "The last few days I've been practicing at home."

"Oh, you have?" Mr. Nichols seemed surprised. "What about pitching?"

Jimmie didn't answer right away. He thought a moment, then said, "I'll tell you about that tomorrow, Mr. Nichols. I have to find out something first."

15

The next morning Jimmie and Ervie went to Paul Karoski's house. It was eleven o'clock. Paul should be home, Jimmie thought. He wanted Ervie along because even though Ervie was a little guy he was somebody. Jimmie didn't want to go alone to see Paul.

He knocked on the front door. His heart beat so loud he could hear it.

The knob turned. The door opened. Mrs. Karoski stood there, her hair in a bun, a comb pressed into it. Her nose wrinkled up as she smiled.

"Jimmie and Ervie Todd!" she cried. "How are you?"

"We're fine, Mrs. Karoski," Jimmie replied. "Is Paul home?"

"Paul?" Mrs. Karoski's smile faded. "Isn't he at your house?"

Jimmie shook his head. "No. Isn't he home?"

Mrs. Karoski lifted her shoulders. "No! Maybe he went to play with somebody else. I don't understand what happened to that boy. Doesn't he play with you anymore?"

Jimmie looked away. "Well — I've been busy practicing baseball. I guess he has, too."

She looked at him curiously. "Don't you play for the same team?"

"No. Paul plays with the Red Rockets. I play with the Planets. That's — that's what I wanted to see him about."

Mrs. Karoski shrugged. "Well, I don't

know where he is. If he comes home soon, I will tell him you're looking for him."

"All right, Mrs. Karoski. Thank you." Jimmie took Ervie's hand. "Let's go to the park," he said. "Maybe he's there."

The park was four blocks away. They walked around the swimming pool, then up the hill to the baseball diamond. Nobody was playing ball. Only two or three kids were around.

"He's not here," Jimmie said. "Let's go to Tiny Zimmer's house. Maybe he's playing catch with Tiny."

But Tiny said he hadn't seen Paul all morning. Why didn't they try some of the other boys' houses? They went to Mose's house, then to Johnny Lukon's, then to Billy Hutt's. They tried every house they thought Paul might possibly go to — but nobody had seen Paul.

"I wonder where he could be, Ervie," Jimmie said worriedly. "Let's go home. Maybe while we were gone he came to our house to see me!"

They hurried home.

"Was anybody here to see me, Mom?" Jimmie asked anxiously.

Mrs. Todd shook her head. "No. But where have you been? Aren't you going to eat lunch?"

"I'm not hungry, Mom," he said, his heart sinking in despair. "We've been looking for Paul Karoski ever since eleven o'clock. He's not home, and he's not at any of the boys' houses we've been to. I think he's lost, Mom."

"Lost in the city? Don't worry. He must be somewhere around. Relax, and eat something. It's after one o'clock."

They crunched on toasted cheese sandwiches and drank a glass of milk each, then went outside again.

Wishy Walters was coming up the walk.

"Hi, Wishy," said Jimmie. "Have you seen Paul Karoski today?"

Wishy thought a moment. "Yes. I saw him this morning."

"You did?" Jimmie's heart cartwheeled. "Where? When?"

"About ten o'clock. He was getting into a car."

"Whose car?"

Wishy shrugged. "I don't know. I wasn't close enough to see."

Jimmie breathed fast. "What color was it? Maybe that'll help."

Wishy thought again. "Brown. No — blue."

"Blue? You sure?"

"Yes. I'm sure. Blue."

"Blue. Blue." Jimmie repeated the word over and over again, trying to think of someone who owned a blue car.

It dawned on him. "Don Perkos!" he shouted. "Don has a blue car! And Don is Paul's cousin! I bet it was his car!"

He ran to the street corner as fast as his legs could carry him.

"Jimmie!" Ervie yelled. "Wait for me!"

"No! You stay there! I'm going to find out if that was Don's car!"

When the light turned green, he ran across the street and down the two blocks to where the Perkos family lived. He stopped in front of the large front door, half out of breath.

Mrs. Perkos answered his knock. She was a tall, thin woman. She looked at Jimmy curiously.

"Mrs. Perkos," Jimmie gasped, "do you know where Don is?"

"Sure," she said. "He went to the lake."

"Which lake?"

She tilted her shoulders. "I don't know. He just told me he was driving to the lake. There are so many lakes around, I don't know which one. I'm sorry."

Jimmie's throat knotted. "Okay. Thank you, Mrs. Perkos."

He walked to Paul's house. "I think that Paul went with his cousin Don," Jimmie said to Mrs. Karoski. "I saw Mrs. Perkos. She said that Don drove to the lake but doesn't know which lake. And Wishy Walters told me he saw Paul get into a blue car. Don has a blue car. That's why I think Paul —"

Mrs. Karoski's eyes filled with tears, and her lips quivered. "Why didn't he tell me where he was going? Why didn't he tell me?" she cried.

Just then a car drove up to the curb. Jimmie turned quickly, hoping to see a blue car.

But it wasn't blue. It was gray.

16

Jimmie recognized the boy in the front seat. His heart jumped. "It's Paul!" he cried.

He leaped down the steps and across the walk. Paul climbed out of the car. He glanced at Jimmie, then looked up at his mother. A smile lighted his face.

"Hi, Mom!" he said.

"Paul!" Mrs. Karoski opened her arms and hugged Paul tightly to her. "Where were you? Four hours you've been gone! Why didn't you tell me you were going some-place?"

"It's my fault, Aunt Josie," Don said. He looked about eighteen. He was neatly dressed, but his black hair was mussed and there was a smudge of grease on his pants. "I was driving to Orange Lake," he explained. "I saw Paul on the street and asked him to come along. I just wanted to drive down and back again. It wouldn't have taken us more than half an hour. That's why I told him he didn't have to run to the house to tell you."

"So what happened?" Mrs. Karoski asked. Tears no longer filled her eyes.

Don shrugged. "We reached the lake, and the car stopped. It wouldn't start again. I wanted to call home, but I couldn't find a telephone. I'm awful sorry, Aunt Josie. I guess I should've had Paul tell you."

Mrs. Karoski said happily, "That's all right. As long as I have my boy back. Next time I think he'd better tell his mother." She kissed Paul's forehead, then held his face between her hands.

"Hungry?" she asked.

"Yes."

"You should be." Mrs. Karoski motioned to Don. "Come inside and bring your friend. There is food for all of you." She paused. "Where is your car now?"

"At the lake. Thanks for asking us to eat, Aunt Josie. But I'm going to see Mom a minute, then get a mechanic to look at my car."

"All right. I hope it's not too expensive to fix."

Don climbed back into the gray car. The young man behind the wheel shifted into gear and they drove off.

Jimmie looked toward the house. Mrs. Karoski was walking in with Paul.

"Hey, Paul!" Jimmie cried. "Just a minute!"

Paul and his mother turned around at the same time. An apologetic look came over Mrs. Karoski's face. "I'm so sorry!" she said. "I forgot you, Jimmie! Come on in!"

"No, thanks, Mrs. Karoski. I just want to ask Paul something." He looked at Paul. "If you want to pitch for the Planets, you can."

For a second Paul looked him straight in the eye. "I'm pitching for the Red Rockets," he said sharply, and walked into the house.

17

Jimmie went home. He felt as if he had lost something.

Ervie was playing with his toys in the backyard. "Did somebody find Paul?" he asked.

"Yes," Jimmie said quietly. "He just got home."

"Did you see him?"

"Yes. He doesn't want to play with us. He's going to stay with the Rockets."

He could hardly say those last words.

"Play with me, will you, Jimmie?" Ervie pleaded.

"Okay. I'll play with you." Anything, Jimmie thought, to forget about Paul.

Ervie had his trucks and steam shovel out. Jimmie operated the steam shovel. He loaded the bucket with sand from a little sand pile, then dumped it into a truck. Ervie pushed the truck across the lawn and dumped it where he had made a road.

Pretty soon Jimmie heard footsteps in the alley. He looked over his shoulder.

"Hi, Mose!" He smiled. "Bring your glove?"

"No." Mose paused in the driveway. "Somebody wants to see you out here, Jimmie."

Jimmie stepped to the edge of the grass. "Who?" he said.

Mose didn't tell him. "Come on," he said. "He's out front."

Jimmie ran to find out who wanted to see him. He heard Ervie running behind him.

At the end of the alley stood Johnny Lukon, Wishy Walters, Billy Hutt, and a couple of other members of the Planets.

In front of them stood — Paul Karoski!

"Hi, Jimmie." Paul smiled.

"Hi, Paul!" Jimmie stared. He could hardly believe his eyes. It seemed a year since Paul had spoken a word to him. A year since Paul had been to see him about anything. "Did — did you want to see me, Paul?"

Paul nodded. "I've changed my mind. I would like to pitch for the Planets," he said.

Jimmie took his hand. "Oh, Paul, I'm so glad! Did you tell all the boys? Is it all right with them?"

"Sure, it's all right," said Wishy. "When I went to see Paul, he told me you were there and asked him. I tried to tell him to come back, too, but he wouldn't listen. So then I brought these guys to his house and we all talked to him."

Jimmie noticed that Ervie was standing beside him, listening to every word, too.

"Paul said the team didn't need two pitchers," Wishy went on. "You wanted to pitch and he wanted to pitch, so when the Red Rockets asked him, he said yes. He felt bad not pitching with us, especially when we lost those games. But he didn't want to tell you — you said you could pitch, and it would look as if he thought you couldn't."

Jimmie choked back an ache in his throat. A chubby hand slipped into his. He gripped it tightly. He was glad Ervie was here. Ervie always made him feel funny when he'd tell a fib to somebody, but at a time like this, Ervie was like a strong pillar he could lean on.

"I know," Jimmie said. "I thought I could pitch. I didn't care what anybody else thought. Johnny tried to tell me. Alan tried to. Even my brother Ervie here tried to. But I wouldn't listen." He took a deep breath. "I had to find out for myself. I'll never make a pitcher, Paul. Never. I'm glad you came back."

"I knew he'd come back," Ervie said, his blue eyes sparkling. "I knew it all the time!"

The boys laughed.

"I'd better call up Mr. Nichols," said Jimmie. "Our first game is Thursday, and the names have to be in before then."

"Better call up Steve Beeler, too. He's the Red Rockets' manager," said Johnny Lukon. "Paul's name can't be on two rosters, or he won't be able to play on either team!"

"That's right!" said Jimmie.

He ran into the house. He telephoned Mr. Nichols and asked him to put Paul Karoski's name on the roster. Mr. Nichols sounded very happy to hear that Paul had changed his mind.

Then Jimmie hesitated. Maybe it would be better if Mr. Nichols telephoned Steve Beeler, he thought.

Jimmie asked him.

"Yes," said Mr. Nichols. "I will do that, Jimmie!"

"Do you think he will mind, Mr. Nichols?"

"You mean about releasing Paul if he has his name on the list?"

"Yes."

"I don't think so. I'll call him. Stay by your phone. I'll let you know as soon as I talk with him."

"Okay, Mr. Nichols."

Jimmie hung up. He sat by the phone, his heart hammering in his chest. If Mr. Beeler would not release Paul, then his hopes would disappear like smoke. The Planets would finish the season in last place.

The phone rang. He picked it up.

"Jimmie? Mr. Nichols again. It's all settled. Paul is now officially a member of the Planets."

18

Paul stretched, looked over his shoulder at the man on first, then threw. The ball sped toward the plate. The batter swung. *Crack!* A hot grounder sizzled across the grass toward short.

Jimmie charged it. He caught the ball on a hop, threw it to second. Kippy caught it, touched the bag, then whipped it to first.

A double play!

"Thataway to play that ball, Jimmie! Way to go, Jimmie!"

Jimmie grinned as the ball sailed around

the horn. He hadn't had so much fun since last year. This was the position for him. He didn't have to throw the ball over the heart of the bag all the time, either. Johnny Lukon's long arms and legs helped him stretch out far enough to catch almost any ball Jimmie threw to him.

It was the first Grasshoppers League game. The Planets were playing the Mohawks. It was the fourth inning and the Planets were leading, 6 to 3. Jimmie remembered the game that the Mohawks had won, 14 to 4. Boy! What a difference it made with Paul on the mound!

Paul liked it with the Planets, too. You could see he was happy the way he stood on the mound, the way he pitched, the way he praised the guys when they hit.

The Mohawks came to bat in the fifth inning. It was their last raps. Their last chance to beat the Planets.

Paul wound up, threw. *Crack!* The ball bounded down short. Jimmie waited for the hop, came up with his glove. But the ball wasn't in it!

His heart sank. He looked behind him. The ball had gone through his legs to the outfield!

A groan lifted from the crowd.

Billy Hutt threw the ball in. Jimmie caught it, glanced at the runner on first, then carried the ball halfway to Paul.

"I'm sorry, Paul," he said, as he tossed it to the left-hander. "I should have had that."

Paul grinned. "Get the next one," he said.

The next batter bunted. The Planets were caught by surprise. Nobody had expected a bunt. The whole infield was playing deep. Everybody was safe.

"Come on, Paul! Come on, kid! Get 'em out of there!" The chatter began.

Men were on first and second. There were

no outs. Paul toed the rubber, looked at the runners, then pitched.

"Ball one!"

The crowd grew tense. Why did I have to miss that ball? thought Jimmie. This would never have happened.

Paul pitched. A line drive to short! Jimmie caught it. He tagged the first runner before the player could get back to second.

"Out!" shrilled the umpire.

Then Jimmie whipped the ball to first to get the second runner before he could tag up. It was close!

The umpire's hands flattened out. "Safe!" he shouted.

Paul struck the next man out.

A loud, air-splitting roar burst from the grandstand. Jimmie ran in toward the mound where Paul was waiting for him, a big happy smile on his face.

"Thataboy, Jimmie! You saved me on that play! That was neat!"

Jimmie was so happy he could shout. Nothing better could have happened to him than making that double play.

The other players came and patted them on the back.

"Thataway, Jimmie!"

"Nice pitching, Paul!"

"I guess we have the team now, don't we!"

A slow smile spread over Jimmie's face.

Winning the game was all right, he thought. But even more important was having Paul back on the team. And as his friend.

The #1
Sports Writer
for Kids

Read them all!